For my son Luke,
always care for what you love. G.F.

minedition
North American edition published 2015 by Michael Neugebauer Publishing Ltd. Hong Kong

Text and Illustrations copyright © 2015 Giuliano Ferri
Originally published by Michael Neugebauer Publishing Ltd., Hong Kong.
Rights arranged with "minedition" Rights and Licensing AG, Zurich, Switzerland.
Michael Neugebauer Publishing Ltd., Unit 23, 7/F, Kowloon Bay Industrial Centre,
15 Wang Hoi Road, Kowloon Bay, Hong Kong. Phone +852 2807 1711,
e-mail: info@minedition.com
This book was printed in January 2015 at L.Rex Printing Co Ltd 3/F., Blue Box Factory
Building, 25 Hing Wo Street, Tin Wan, Aberdeen, Hong Kong, China
Typesetting in Big Caslon
Color separation by Pixelstorm, Vienna
Library of Congress Cataloging-in-Publication Data available upon request.

ISBN 978-988-8240-94-4

10 9 8 7 6 5 4 3 2 1
First Impression

For more information please visit our website: www.minedition.com

Luke & the Little Seed

Giuliano Ferri

minedition

It was Luke's birthday.
Everyone brought presents.
What a wonderful day it was!

His grandfather gave him a little bag.

"What's inside?" asked Luke.

"Open the bag and see," said Grandfather.

"Oh," said Luke, "it's just seeds."

"Well," said Grandfather, "plant one and see what grows. If you take care of it, it will turn into a very exciting gift. Not only will it feed you, but you'll be able to play in its branches too!"

Luke could hardly believe Grandfather's promise.
What mysterious gift could this seed be?
Off he went with his grandfather, and they planted the seed
and gave it a little water. Luke went to sleep that night full of
excitement for what he would discover the next day.

The next morning Luke ran to the garden.
But nothing had happened at all.
"It must be a joke," he said.
"Not at all," said Grandfather, "but give it time. You must water it every day and wait.
The most important thing is to be patient. You'll see."

Luke looked at the ground where he had planted the seed.
Waiting was dull, but he was curious to see if his grandfather
was right. He took his watering can and gave it some water.
Every day Luke watered his seed. Nothing happened.
"This is so boring!" he complained.
"Be patient," said Grandfather.

And then one morning, Luke ran into the garden and there was something growing! But it wasn't anything he could play with and certainly not much to eat.

But Grandfather said, "Well done, Luke. Keep taking care of it and you won't be disappointed."

Every day Luke gave the leaf some water. Three, then four days passed but there didn't seem to be much happening.

Luke's friends asked him to come with them to swim in the river.

"I can't," said Luke, "I have my plant to look after."

"Oh, do it later!" they said.

And when Luke came home he was so tired that he forgot to water it.

In the morning Luke woke up and remembered he had
forgotten to do his watering. He ran to the garden and
found his plant was limp and the earth was dry.

"Is it dead?" he asked Grandfather.

"I don't know," said Grandfather.

"We'll find out tomorrow."

"I'm sorry," said Luke to his little plant.

"It's all my fault. I promise I won't forget you again."

The next day Luke ran to his garden.
The plant looked fine after all!
After that he looked after it carefully – every day.
And his friends came to see it, too, and they admired
how it was growing.

Then one day Luke woke up sneezing.
He didn't feel well, and his mother said he should go back to bed.
"But Mom, I can't, my plant needs me!"
Luke's good friends kindly looked after his plant for him.
When he asked his grandfather how it was growing, he was told,
"Don't worry, Luke, your friends are taking care of it."

At last, Luke could get up. He ran to his garden. And what did he see? His little seed had grown into a beautiful tomato plant, tall, with many leaves and bright red tomatoes shining in the sun!

Grandfather said, "Try one!" Luke picked one and tried it. "Wow!" he said. "This is the best tomato I have ever eaten."

Luke invited all his friends to try some too.
And then they played all day in the tomato plant,
sliding and swinging on the stalks and every so
often stopping to eat one of the juicy tomatoes.
When evening came Luke thanked his grandfather.
"What a wonderful gift," he said, "the most wonderful
gift of my life."
"Yes," said Grandfather, "and together we made it
happen, didn't we, Luke?"